Fifties

A Justin Deming
Literary Project

Justin Deming

Copyright © 2023 by Justin Deming

All rights reserved. No part of this publication may be reproduced or transmitted in any form or by any means, electronic or otherwise, without written permission from the author.

Cover design by John Lightle

Book design by Meg Oolders

"Grandpa Al" was originally published in 50-Word Stories.

Proudly self-published.

Visit jdeming.com for more.

ISBN: 9798869872753

*To my grandmothers,
Doris and Patricia,
for filling my life with stories.*

Introduction

On a cold December morning, back in 2018, I found myself rummaging through my parents' garage while home for the holidays. To this day, I don't know what possessed me to do it. Upstate New York in the wintertime is beyond frigid, and I rarely went out to the garage to begin with because I was never much of a tinkerer.

I came across an old, dusty chest on a high shelf. It had belonged to my grandparents. When I opened the chest and began rifling through some of the papers it contained, I was stunned.

It felt like I had stepped through a portal into the past.

Countless handwritten poems, songs, and lyrics stared up at me, all of which had been written by my Grandpa Alden, or Al, for short. He had even written letters to music producers, requesting them to consider his work. Most of the material had been written in the 1950s—some of it while he was fighting overseas in the Korean War.

I don't know how long I remained in the garage, hunched over, poring through these family heirlooms. At some point I felt the sting of tears, felt the deep connection with my grandfather through time, space, and life and death itself.

He had been a writer, too.

I never knew that about him—never knew his head was in the clouds, like mine.

Soon after this experience, I wrote one of my first fifty-word stories, or *fifties*, as I like to call them now. I titled it "Grandpa Al" and submitted it to a small, online publisher. Sure enough, it was accepted and published on New Year's Day, 2019.

At the time, I didn't realize this experience would impact my writing life in such a profound way.

To put it bluntly, I fell in love with the fifty-word form of storytelling.

After finding some success with building a writing community over at Medium from 2019-2020 (I ran a publication called *The Friday Fix*, which focused on fifty-word stories), I decided to revamp my process and share some of my other short-form fiction through a new platform, Substack.

As of September 2022, I have been hosting biweekly writing prompts at *Along the Hudson*, my fiction newsletter. The series is called "Fifties by the Fire", and writers are tasked with creating fifty-word stories based on a single prompt.

After personally writing hundreds of these pocket-sized stories, I finally decided to compile fifty of my favorites and self-publish them.

With the help of my brilliant photographer friend, John Lightle, and fellow fiction writing pal and book designer, Meg Oolders, I've been able to bring this dream to fruition.

May I present to you, dear reader, *50 Fifties*.

<u>1</u>

Inhaling Her

Blaise watched his wife from the cabana. She waded ankle-deep in the Caribbean, collecting seashells—a perfect memory.

When he gulped the thin mountain air, trapped in an icy crevasse, he inhaled her. Hypothermic, somewhere above Camp Four, he'd surely die. But the summer breeze would take him home.

2

The Woeful Farmer

When the lightning danced across the sky and the deep thrum of thunder carried out across the plains for the fifth night in a row, he knew the end had come.

Torrents of rain and softball-sized hail pounded all around him, devastating his crops, ripping through them like swinging scythes.

3

Ancient Secret

Royce left the city.

When he found himself planted in the heart of the Adirondacks, something came over him. The wilderness took hold of his body, forcing him to take it in—the mountains, the trees, the sky.

A gust of wind swept through, revealing an ancient secret: *you're home*.

4

Billy's Hubcap Heaven

The sign out front clatters against the chain link fence. Mountains of hubcaps, rusted-out cars, and scrap metal litter the property. Billy doesn't see the mess. He sees art, history—an empire forming and expanding. He sits on the hood of his dead blue Camaro and smiles.

5

Time

He looked high, low—everywhere.

For years he searched in unlikely places, always hoping the truth would rear its ugly head.

On his deathbed, he called his children close: he had finally found it.

"Time," he whispered. "It's all we'll ever have."

Though his had ended, the moment spanned eternity.

6

A Newfound World

After winter's thaw, two sisters muddied their sneakers as they hiked through the woods. One halted. "Forests are like libraries," she whispered.

"Why?" the other asked.

"They're quiet. And you can learn a lot here."

They walked on, fascinated by this newfound world—this beautiful discovery in their backyard.

7

Soaking It In

Uncle Joe loved the rain.

It was only fitting that on the day of his funeral the skies opened up. As the trumpeter played "Taps" and umbrellas flipped inside out from the whipping wind, I knew without a doubt he was smiling, laughing down at us—soaking it all in.

8

Alive

He was trapped inside his own body and mind—the world obscured in a dark shroud of mystery.

But when he heard music, everything came alive in bright landscapes of color. Mountains, forests, and oceans appeared before him, breaking his chains, sweeping him into this alternate reality—this immaculate universe.

9

Open Mic

Tre rapped about his life. Paul plucked guitar strings, telling a different version of the same tale. After the open mic closed for the night, the two men swapped stories at the bar, connecting over their shared fates: both orphans, both dropouts, both directionless until they found meaning through music.

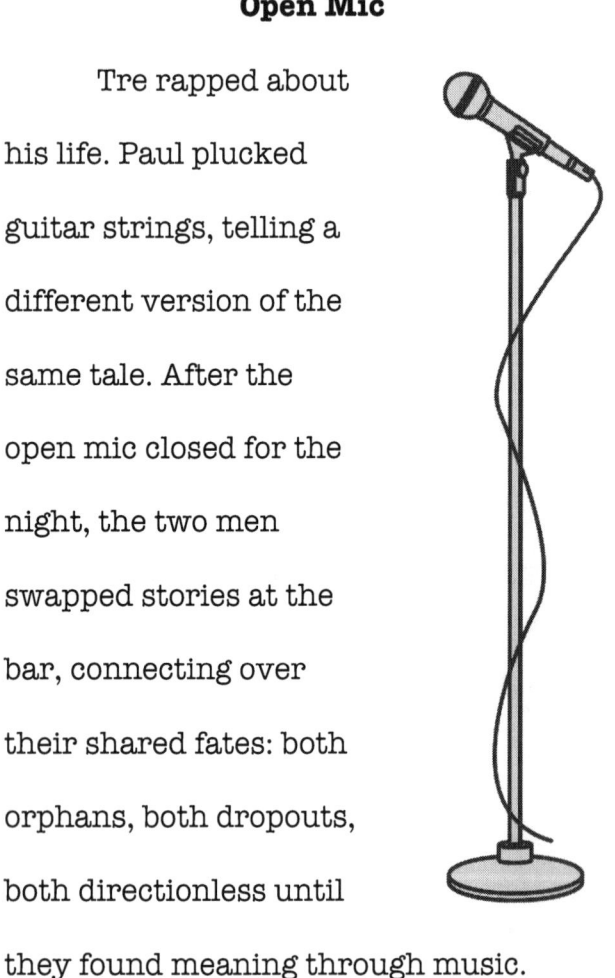

__10__

Purgatory

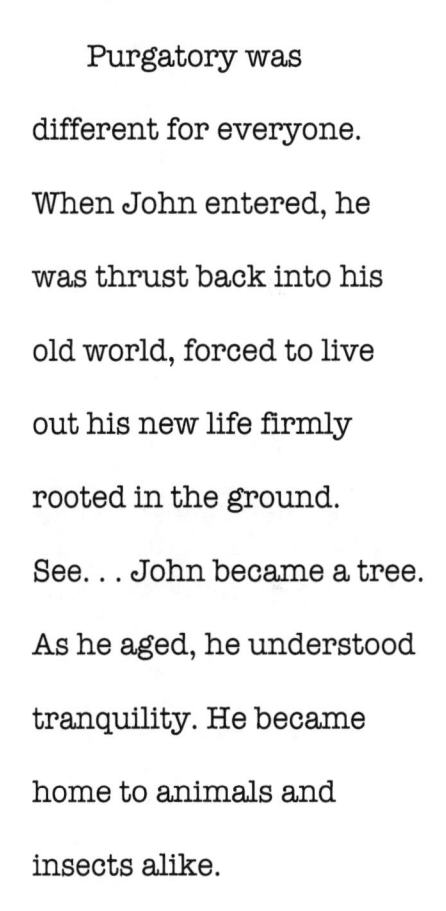

Purgatory was different for everyone. When John entered, he was thrust back into his old world, forced to live out his new life firmly rooted in the ground. See. . . John became a tree. As he aged, he understood tranquility. He became home to animals and insects alike.

He still stands.

__11__

Contemplation

The battle-hardened men of the past gaze at us in silent contemplation through clouds of cigarette smoke. The lines on their faces are like medals of honor—wrinkled badges of courage. I run a hand across my own, feel the smooth surface, and wonder if I'd have it in me.

12

Nothing Happened

Davey wandered barefoot along the abandoned railroad tracks behind his family's trailer—almost stepped on a busted bottle of *Jack*.

He walked until he stumbled upon an old, engraved sign in the woods:

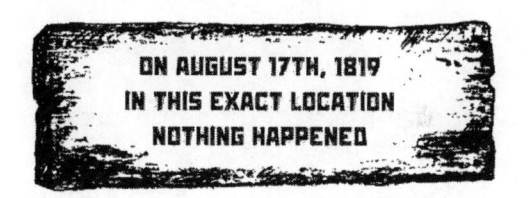

> ON AUGUST 17TH, 1819
> IN THIS EXACT LOCATION
> NOTHING HAPPENED

Davey snorted—almost laughed—then headed home.

13

Believer

"Do you believe in ghosts?" the woman asked the man at the bar. Everyone wore Halloween costumes.

"No, I don't think I do. You?"

She grinned. "I died in a fire in 1913." Her face morphed. Flesh bubbled and burned.

He dropped his drink and ran like hell.

14

William

William lived alone; everyone he loved was gone. That's what happens when you make it to ninety-seven.

As snow fell on Christmas Eve, he woke with a start. The love of his life, Eleanor, stood before him. So did the rest of his family.

William smiled, the world turning white.

15

The Greatest Gift

Paula and Martin couldn't afford presents this year; they wrote each other stories and poems instead. The newlyweds rolled up their creations and placed them carefully in the tree.

They spent Christmas day laughing and crying as they reflected, reminisced—dreamed.

In the end, their greatest gift was each other.

__16__

The Train Hopper

Milo hopped aboard the westward-bound freight train under the cover of darkness. He slipped inside a boxcar. Moonlight glimmered on his face.

"Hey," a seasoned, smoky voice called from the shadows. "Where you heading, kid?"

"I don't know."

"No? Well, where you from?"

"Nowhere."

The man's voice cracked. "Me too."

__17__

Never Again

They lived a quiet, simple existence in the cabin. The forest, a meadow, and red foxes were their neighbors.

Edith prepared supper every night while James tended to the woodstove or read the paper.

One night, it dawned on him: *We're running out of time.*

She never cooked alone again.

18

Lost Soul

He finds the fabled pool—the ancient abalone.

"Please," the man begs. "I wish for a better life."

In an instant, he's compressed, morphed, and blown away in the wind. He lands, joins brothers and sisters—fellow lost souls.

A sapling begins to grow near the edge of a forest.

19

Unconquerable

"Go—creep into the world. Set fear in their hearts. Strike hard and fast in the East!" Death ordered her loyal followers as they set out on the warpath. The initial attack was essential.

Soon, the pandemic engulfed the world. But the tide shifted; normalcy returned.

Human spirit proved unconquerable.

20

The Question

He knew she would say yes. She *would* say yes . . . right? When he asked her on a moonlit beach, minutes from their shoddy apartment, the response was muted by crashing waves—completely muffled by the powerful sea.

Later, alone, they twirled in the blackened night, their only witnesses the stars.

21

Tammy Two-Socks

When Tammy Two-Socks turned seven years old, she finally stopped sucking her thumb.

"Thank the Lord," her father said, tired of sending the poor kid off to bed with socks on her hands.

Before he had a moment's peace, his son growled and came into view, crawling on all fours.

22

The Lighter

In September, Mr. Rodriguez caught Tre with a lighter in the boys' bathroom. He confiscated it.

Tre challenged him all year. He interrupted his lessons—even got into a shouting match.

One day in June, Tre held out his hand. "Thanks, man."

Mr. Rodriguez pulled his student into a hug.

23

Sewn Shut

"His eyes are sewn shut," Marc whispered. "Don't move. He'll hear you."

The three boys quieted as the monster crept through the woods. Tree branches snapped. Leaves rustled.

Silence.

"Raaa!" The monster jumped out and tried to devour the others.

"Get back to base!" Marc exclaimed, inhaling sweet summer air.

24

Final Step

The wolf takes its final step,

crumpling onto the hard-packed earth.

The animal gazes glassy eyed as a

vast horde of translucent beasts wanders

closer. Even his former companion—the

kind, older man with the beard and

blade—limps toward the wolf.

"Come here, Keno. It's time to go

home."

25

History Lingers

The old house, with its wildly overgrown garden, is silent, secretive.

Long abandoned.

History lingers in the rose bushes and dilapidated walls—even the chills that cut through human flesh.

"Snap your photographs, fool," Lucille whispers in the young man's ear. "Then *leave*!"

But all he feels is the wind.

26

Torn

She had a choice: the sun, moon, or stars.

Ultimately her decision wouldn't matter. He'd never give these gifts to her.

She settled on the sun, but he stole it—locked it in a dark closet and hid the key.

The day she left, it came back, bright as diamonds.

27

Between Worlds

When he came to his senses, he found himself floating in a black limitless space. Perhaps the disease had finally won.

"Is this heaven?" he whispered. He swam upward in this strange new realm, bypassing gigantic jellyfish. They followed after him, lighting the way.

His life's journey had only begun.

28

Lisbeth

Lisbeth haunted the fields surrounding her old home.

She never understood why he murdered her. He'd always been a father figure, a mentor, a coach—someone she had trusted.

At night you can still hear her from town, shrieking at the blood-red moon, the unrelenting dark: "*Why, why, why?*"

29

Colliding Worlds

She was a river girl, and he was a mountain man. When they met in the storm, they both knew their worlds had collided at exactly the right time.

In short, he became the river, and she the mountain. They bore children, the forests, blanketed by sky and clouds above.

30

Magic

They told us we couldn't go. The man was dangerous—he knew magic.

We left town at midnight. Our hearts fluttered as we crept past the broken bridge—an ogre's home.

When we reached the outcast's book-strewn hut, he let us in.

That night, we learned the power of words.

31

The Rest is History

Time stood still.

He saw her from across the way.

She wore a sky-blue summer dress, which seemed to bring out her striking eyes even more. Her hair was braided.

Typically a wallflower, Quentin approached her. He couldn't let the moment pass.

The rest is, as they say, history.

32

Gold Gone

Winston Jones was the fastest sprinter in the world.

He qualified for the Olympics, breezed through the initial heats, and found himself standing at the starting line of the most important race of his life.

But Winston jumped before the gun.

Dream crushed, gold gone, he was escorted off the track.

33

A Siren's Call

She whispered melodies and spoke in symphonies. Her voice carried out across the water, stopping all travelers within earshot.

Ships rocked against the shoreline—some abandoned for centuries.

The island was peaceful, mountainous, and desolate. The men who wandered there were trapped under her spell, pawns in her grand scheme.

34

Seeking Silence

Screaming at the world never worked for Jamir.

He grew older and learned the importance of listening, a gentle tone, and seeking silence. There was something profound in simplicity. This forgotten temple became his sanctuary. He found friendships in the unlikeliest of places; he discovered love.

Jamir considered himself blessed.

35

Priorities

Exhausted at the end of the night, Joseph and Janell gaze at their disorderly apartment.

Dirty stacks of dishes rise out of the sink. Unpaid bills and unread magazines litter the countertops. Laundry and toys lie everywhere.

But the children are asleep, content and dreaming. Everything will be all right.

36

The Cardinal

Chelsea James visits her children every spring.

This year she returns in the form of a cardinal. She lands on a high branch overlooking the backyard. All three children laugh as they play soccer. Her husband gazes up at her, watching intently.

She takes him in, chirps, and flies home.

37

Two Horses

Viera walks straight into the fencepost and grunts. Angelo nuzzles against the blind mare and then guides her toward the water buckets, nudging her every step of the way.

Viera finds the water and drinks; the younger stallion stays beside her the whole time.

Summer wind whips through their manes.

38

Pep Talk

Hold on. Come here—take a deep breath.

Listen.

Do you hear that? All that noise?

Block it out, all of it—everything.

You're only going to get one shot at this. People are going to remember this moment. How do you want your story to end?

Go write it.

39

Voicemail

Sheila keeps a single voicemail saved on her phone. It's the final recording she received from her father.

"Hey, kiddo. Just figured I'd try reaching ya...I'm sure I'll talk to you later. Love ya."

His tone still calms her when she needs him most.

A parent's love knows no bounds.

40

Wings

Natalia was born with wings.

Her parents hid her away from the world, afraid of what others might say.

At five years old, she attended school and was mocked for her differences.

When she learned to fly, her classmates quieted, took her in—saw her clearly for the first time.

41

First Snowfall

Every winter, the first snowfall reminds Monique of her husband. She remembers the phone call, the accident—pulling up to the scene. But then she sees his smile, hears his voice—gets engulfed in his arms.

"I love you, honey," she whispers into the cold.

The wind swirls in response.

42

She

She was the favorite season of his life.

Late nights, early mornings: always hitting the road on an adventure. Working on the fly and making money when needed. Two years in, she grew tired of it all—wanted something sure, something stable.

When winter arrived, it took hold, lingering forever.

43

Times Change

but the Song Remains the Same

Melissa remembers when her father tucked her in at night. He read books, told stories, and even sang. "Blackbird" by the Beatles comes to mind. His voice was deep, melodic.

Now it's her turn. She tucks him in, kisses his bald, wrinkled head, and hums the same tune.

He smiles.

44

Riptide

The Atlantic needed to feed.

Jamie had been swimming in its shallows when the riptide pulled him under. He tried powering through—fighting against its force—but it proved hopeless. Thinking quickly, he swam parallel to the coast. He inhaled saltwater, tasted death. Saw light, life—broke free, sputtering.

Freedom.

45

Cataclysm

Yellowstone erupted on a calm Sunday morning.

"Daddy, when will the ash go away?" Max asked as we fled east.

I choked on words. Nothing came out. On the seventeenth night, stars reappeared. We held each other—hugged strangers in our impromptu roadside camp.

A small sliver of hope remained.

46

Language Barriers

Raul was new. He didn't speak English; Rebecca knew little Spanish.

Rebecca reviewed roots and stems, common nouns, and verbs. Tenses. Raul worked hard and followed his tutor's instructions. The two high schoolers often laughed together.

One day, Raul brought her flowers. She kissed him. Maybe words weren't always needed.

47

First Heartbreak

"I can't believe she dumped me on Valentine's Day, Dad."

"Come on," the father said to his son. "I've got an idea."

They slung their old ice skates and hockey sticks over their shoulders, then headed through the snowy forest to the pond.

The puck passed between them for hours.

48

New World

This is the house that saved us.

We were passing through—on our way to Albuquerque—when the first bombs fell. The doomsayer poked his head outside and waved us in emphatically.

Months later we emerge to a world of ash and ruin.

For some reason, we choose to rebuild.

49

A Whirl Through Time

The whirlpool appeared before us.

It was a monster. A calamity.

It pulled our ship into its current,

then forced us into the downward spiral.

We prayed. Cried.

Yet water didn't fill our ship—our

lungs.

We emerged on a coastline with

tall, leafy trees.

A Brachiosaurus turned its head.

50

Grandpa Al

Grandpa Al radioed coordinates during the Korean War. He was quiet, loved his Yankees, and sipped O'Doul's in the summertime. He had a fake leg and owned a ukulele, too—a sweet, beautiful instrument boxed up in his basement.

I can see him now.

He's smiling. Sipping. Strumming and plucking.

Acknowledgements

First and foremost, I must thank my family. To my wife, Courtney, for supporting me in my writing endeavors from day one—thank you. You are the center of my universe. And to my children, Dakota and Cooper, for keeping the spirit of creativity and imagination alive on a daily basis. Daddy loves you.

Thank you to my parents and my brother, Aaron, for their unwavering support over the years. You have no idea how impactful you've all been.

I'm forever grateful for photographer John Lightle's feedback and guidance throughout this process. (Not to mention the stunning cover!) And I can't mention John without mentioning Meg Oolders. Meg is an incredibly talented fiction writer, and she also had an immaculate eye and vision for shaping the overall design of this book. Thank you both. I couldn't have asked for a better team to work with.

Special thanks to my dear friend and editor, Andrea Tackach. Andrea has helped me in more ways than one, and I'm indebted to her for helping me with this project.

I've been fortunate to have crossed paths with so many talented writers over the past few years. I could fill pages with names, but I'll do my best to remain brief. Thanks to the following for their support and encouragement: Mark Starlin, Dascha Paylor, Jenise Cook, Jimmy Doom, Sharron Bassano, Amie McGraham, Bill Adler, Brian Reindel, Jason McBride, Jim Latham, and Kim Smyth. To all I left out: you know you who you are.

Lastly, thank you, dear reader, for choosing to pick up a copy of *50 Fifties*. I hope these stories resonated with you and impacted you in some small way. I'd love to have you aboard this writing journey with me at *Along the Hudson*, my Substack publication. Perhaps you'll even stop by the fire to read and write some fifties.

Until then, be well.

Justin
December 2023

If you would like to read more of my fiction, or join an ever-expanding writing community, please visit *Along the Hudson*.

About the Design Team

John Lightle works outside of convention. It allows him to build gardens, write poetry, play guitar, and work his camera. He travels around Texas as an art show vendor, which has led to publication, winning awards, being featured in public art displays, and a solo gallery exhibit. He lives in Plano, leaving the rest of the world as a playground.

Meg Oolders is the author of the Watty Award winning YA novel *See Dot Smile* and the creator of the edgy short fiction Substack publication, *Stock Fiction*. Her background includes decades of fulfilling work in theater, music, and culinary arts, but her greatest passion has always been writing. She is grateful for any opportunity to share her gifts, and collaborate with fellow artists, while on a mission to leave her mark on the world, by any creative means necessary.

About the Author

Justin Deming lives and teaches in the Hudson Valley region of New York. His work has appeared in *Spelk*, *Flash Fiction Magazine*, *Emerge Literary Journal*, and elsewhere. He writes weekly fiction and hosts "Fifties by the Fire" at *Along the Hudson*, his Substack newsletter. More of his stories can be found at jdeming.com.